Get to know the girls of

BY
CHRISSIE PERRY

ILLUSTRATED BY
ASH OSWALD

SQUARE
FISH

FEIWEL AND FRIENDS
NEW YORK

⊣⊢
SQUARE
FISH

An imprint of Macmillan Publishing Group, LLC
175 Fifth Avenue
New York, NY 10010
mackids.com

Our books may be purchased in bulk for promotional, educational,
or business use. Please contact your local bookseller or the
Macmillan Corporate and Premium Sales Department
at (800) 221-7945 ext. 5442 or by e-mail at
MacmillanSpecialMarkets@macmillan.com.

Library of Congress Cataloging-in-Publication Data Available

ISBN 978-1-250-11542-3 (paperback)

Originally published in Australia by E2, an imprint of
Hardie Grant Egmont.
Illustration and design by Ash Oswald
First published in the United States by Feiwel and Friends
First U.S. Edition: 2008
Square Fish Reissue Edition: 2017
Square Fish logo designed by Filomena Tuosto

1   3   5   7   9   10   8   6   4   2

AR: 3.7

CHAPTER ONE

Lucy dragged her yellow surfboard into the bathroom and put it in the tub. Her big sister Frankie was getting ready to go out. She was looking in the mirror, putting brown sludge on her face.

Lucy knew it was makeup, and that it was supposed to make Frankie look better, but Lucy secretly thought Frankie was much prettier without it.

"Hey, Lucy Lou," said Frankie. "I can't see any waves in that bathtub."

Lucy grinned. It *was* kind of silly to take the board everywhere she went, but she couldn't help it.

Lucy had left hints all around the house before Christmas. She'd put a picture of the surfboard she wanted on the fridge under a magnet. She had even put a picture under her mom's pillow, so she could sleep on the idea. And the hints had worked! Lucy still couldn't believe she had her very own surfboard.

"Actually, I do know there aren't any waves in the bathtub," Lucy said. "It's just that I'm *so* excited about going on a surfing

trip with Bonnie."

She lifted the board out of the tub and swung it around. It almost hit Frankie's head.

"Do you know Bonnie has a board, too?" Lucy asked, stroking the board.

"Hers is red. We're going to be surfer girls together. We'll paddle through the water and ride the big waves. I can't wait!"

"Well, you don't have to wait long," Frankie said. "Bonnie's parents will be here soon."

Lucy's heart fluttered, as though she was high on a swing. It was *so cool* to be going away on a beach vacation with her best friend. Lucy and Bonnie had been talking about it for ages. And Bonnie's parents, Ross and Helen, had already booked surfing lessons for them. They would have five whole days to learn how to become surfer girls.

But Lucy knew that five days and five

nights was a long time to be away from her mom, dad, and Frankie.

Her longest school trip had only been for two days and one night. That had been all right, except when Mr. Halliday had tried to get her to eat broccoli.

Five days is a long time to be away.

Lucy *hated* broccoli. When she put it in her mouth, she felt like she was going to throw up. Lucy didn't just feel sick, she felt sad. It was as though the broccoli hit a little button in her throat, and started an attack of homesickness. Luckily, Mr. Halliday didn't make her take a second bite.

What if Ross and Helen served broccoli for every meal? Broccoli cereal, broccoli pudding, broccoli cake . . .

Bonnie had twin brothers, Shane and Tom. What if broccoli was their favorite food?

"Earth to Lucy. Earth to Lucy. Come in, Lucy," Frankie snapped her fingers in Lucy's face. "Are you OK?" she asked.

"Yep, I'm fine," Lucy replied, though she wasn't quite so sure now.

Frankie started walking down the hallway. Lucy followed, dragging the surfboard behind her. It made a squeaking sound on the floorboards.

"Is that the cat?" Lucy's mom called from the kitchen.

"No, Mom. It's just Lucy and the you-know-what," Frankie called back.

Lucy stared at the stickers on Frankie's bedroom door.

The message was pretty clear.

"Well, see you in five days," Lucy said. She let out a little sigh.

Frankie rolled her eyes.

"OK, Lou, you can come in just this once," Frankie said, pushing open her bedroom door. "But the board stays out there."

It was pretty weird to be invited into

Frankie's room. Lucy sometimes snuck in there when Frankie was out, but this was different. Frankie sat in front of her dressing table. Lucy sat on the bed. She could see Frankie in the mirror.

"So, what's the problem?" Frankie asked, as she looked at a pimple on her chin. Frankie tried to cover it up with more sludge.

"I don't really have a problem," Lucy said. "I'm just going to miss you guys."

Frankie nodded. She reached into her dresser drawer and pulled out a small black book with a lock and key.

She threw it to Lucy.

"What's this?" Lucy asked.

"It's a diary, you dummy," Frankie said.

"For me?"

"Yeah. I've already got one. You can take this one away with you. You can write about whatever happens on your vacation. Then you won't be lonely."

"Do you think I'll have anything interesting enough to write about in a diary?" Lucy asked.

Frankie rolled her eyes again. She really seemed to like doing that.

"Listen, Lou. You can write about anything you want in a diary. It doesn't have to be all about stuff that happens— you can write about your feelings, too. I write about lots of different things in my diary. It's cool. It's like letting your thoughts escape out of your head and onto the paper."

"Thanks," said Lucy, opening the diary with the little key and staring at the blank pages. It was hard to imagine how she would be able to fill up this whole book. She wondered what Frankie had written in hers. Probably a lot of stuff about her new boyfriend. That would *definitely* be interesting.

Just then, a car horn beeped.

"Got to go," Frankie said, standing up.

She grabbed Lucy by the shoulders and steered her out into the hallway.

"Hey, Frankie, can I read your diary?"

asked Lucy. "It might give me some ideas about what to put in mine."

Frankie rolled her eyes again, but this time she laughed.

"Don't push your luck, Lou," she said.

CHAPTER TWO

When the Prestons arrived to pick up Lucy, their car was packed with vacation stuff. Lucy and Bonnie sat in the backseat, behind Bonnie's brothers.

"Check out Block and Pin," Bonnie whispered, pointing at her brothers. The boys were asleep in the middle seats. "Shane is the Blockhead and Tom is the Pinhead," Bonnie half sung and half whispered.

"They don't look like twins, do they?" said Lucy, giggling.

"Look at Shane's huge head. It's about ten times bigger than Tom's," said Bonnie.

It *was* hard to believe they were twins. Shane was big and blond, and Tom was dark-haired and very thin. Shane was dribbling just a tiny bit, and his blockhead bumped against the window. Tom's pinhead was crumpled against Shane's leg. Tom was snoring very loudly for such a little guy.

"Hey, watch this," Bonnie said. She tore off a tiny piece of tissue, and placed it gently on Tom's nose. As Tom breathed out, the tissue flew around the car. Lucy leaned against Bonnie and laughed.

Bonnie was fantastic. She could even make a boring car trip fun!

Soon, they arrived at the beach. It was all so blue, Lucy could hardly tell where the water stopped and the sky began.

This summer vacation is going to rock!

Bonnie rolled down the window and the salt air rushed in. Lucy reached for her sunglasses so she could see where Bonnie was pointing.

"That's the beach shack. They sell the best burgers and fries in the world. And over there are the trampolines. And that's the ice cream truck!" Bonnie raved.

"Wow," said Lucy. "This is awesome!"

She took a deep breath. It was like a whole new world out there.

"OK, kids," said Bonnie's dad, parking the car. "Grab your suits and towels. Let's get down there and enjoy the day. We can unpack later."

Lucy ran along the sand with the others. Shane and Tom ran into the water between the flags and dived straight under. Bonnie went ahead of Lucy and dived in, too.

Lucy preferred to get in slowly. She waited until her ankles were used to the freezing cold water, then she walked in up to her knees. When her knees felt OK, she walked in up to her hips.

Suddenly, Tom appeared in front of her. He took big scoops of water and whooshed them towards her. Lucy gasped as the cold water splashed her.

"That's for putting tissues up my nose," he yelled.

"We thought you were asleep!" Lucy squealed. The water tingled and fizzed as it hit her tummy.

"A-ha! Maybe that's what I wanted you to think," Tom said.

Just then, Lucy noticed Tom had something behind his back.

Seaweed!

"Bonnie—help!" she screamed. "Pinhead is attacking!"

Next thing she knew, Bonnie was in front of her. She spread her arms and legs wide, protecting Lucy from Tom.

"Dive under," Bonnie yelled. "Then it doesn't matter if he splashes you."

Lucy couldn't stop grinning. This vacation was going to be the most fun ever. And Bonnie was the best friend ever. She was always there when Lucy needed her.

"Hurry! Dive," Bonnie called over her shoulder.

Lucy held her breath. She held her nose with her fingers and went backwards into the water. When she came up, she was wearing a seaweed necklace.

"Hey, you look like a mermaid," Bonnie said.

"More like a sea monster," Tom said.

They all started laughing and splashing again. Lucy knew that she was going to have lots of interesting things to write in her diary.

CHAPTER THREE

The next morning, Lucy and Bonnie walked along the sand to their surfing class.

"The grommets' beginner class is over there," said one of the surfing teachers.

"I'm not going with any grommets," Bonnie said to Lucy. "They sound gross."

"Bonnie, grommets are young surfers!" Lucy whispered.

"Oh, I knew *that*," said Bonnie.

They took off their flip-flops. The sand was hot. They had to move quickly to stop it from burning their feet, but running in a wetsuit felt very weird. Lucy felt as though she was covered in millions of layers of Saran Wrap.

Lucy and Bonnie's instructor was named Luke. Luke introduced them to the other two girls in their class.

"This is Karen," said Luke. "And this is Mia."

Lucy liked the look of Karen. She had bright blue eyes and an even brighter smile. It was hard to tell what Mia looked like. She kept her head down, and didn't even say hello. Lucy thought she was very rude.

After Luke explained some safety rules, the four girls lay on their boards in the sand. They had to practice jumping up from their bellies and onto their knees. Lucy thought it was really easy, even though her wetsuit felt a little too tight.

Finally, it was time to go into the ocean. They stood in the surf up to their knees.

"It's good to practice your surfing here," Luke said. "The waves have already broken, so the water is moving, but not too fast."

Lucy looked out to where the big waves were breaking. Shane was standing up on his board, riding the barrel of a wave. Tom was out kind of far, too, but he seemed to spend most of his time lying on his stomach or falling off his board.

Lucy put her board down in the water, and tried to kneel on top of it. The sea was cold on her ankles, where the wetsuit stopped. She put one knee on the board, and toppled off.

It was really very different from practicing on the sand. It felt like she was trying to stand up on a mound of wobbly jelly.

"Hey, look at me!" Bonnie shouted. She kneeled on her board for about five seconds, and then nose-dived into the water.

Lucy laughed, and tried to get up again. This time she fell into the water headfirst.

A stream of salt water gushed up her nostrils. Even then, she couldn't stop laughing. Karen put out her hand so Lucy could steady herself.

Mia just stood in the surf and stared at them. She didn't seem to be trying any of the moves Luke was teaching.

Argh!

Lucy decided that she didn't like Mia very much.

"Put your knees like this," Luke called out. He put his hands on the board to show them where their knees should be.

By the end of the lesson, Bonnie managed to kneel for thirty seconds. Lucy managed to nose-dive about thirty times! She felt like she had swallowed half of the ocean, but it had been fun.

"Ice cream time," Bonnie said, as they peeled off their wetsuits and slathered on sunscreen.

Shane and Tom were already at the window of the ice cream truck.

"How did you do?" Shane asked. He had three flavors on a double cone. Lucy wondered whether he could get through it all before it melted.

"It was *wicked*," Bonnie said. "I think I'll be able to stand up tomorrow."

"Huh, then you might be able to teach Tom," Shane teased. "He spends most of his time down with the fishies."

Shane sucked in the corners of his mouth, making fish lips.

Bonnie giggled, but Tom didn't seem to think it was funny.

"What do you guys want?" Shane asked.

"I'll have what you're having—chocolate, vanilla, and strawberry in a double cone," Bonnie said excitedly.

"I'll just have vanilla in a single cone," Tom said quietly.

"Me, too," said Lucy, smiling at Tom.

CHAPTER FOUR

Later that evening, Lucy, Bonnie, and her brothers went down to the beach shack to order burgers and fries for everyone.

As they walked back up the hill to the vacation house, Shane strode ahead, carrying the burgers and fries. Bonnie jogged to keep up with him, even though the hill was steep and Shane was walking really fast. Lucy and Tom walked behind them.

Shane and Bonnie had already opened the bag of food and were pulling out delicious hot fries.

"Hey, no fair!" Tom called out.

Shane dangled a fry from his fingers. "Come and get one then," he teased.

Tom and Lucy ran ahead, but as soon as the fry was just within reach, Shane and Bonnie would run off again.

"Those two are *so* greedy," Lucy said.

As soon as she'd spoken, she felt bad. It wasn't a very nice thing to say about her best friend.

"Worse than seagulls," Tom agreed. "Come on, we'd better get back or there will be nothing left."

Lucy grinned. Tom was OK.

Soon, the whole family was sitting on the porch eating the yummiest burgers and fries Lucy had ever tasted.

After dinner, all the kids went into the playroom.

"Where's the TV?" Lucy asked.

"There isn't one," Bonnie said. "But there *is* a CD player. Let's put on a concert!"

The boys groaned.

"Oh, come on," Bonnie urged. "Lucy is great at making up dances. She has the *best* moves!"

"I'm not *that* good," Lucy said, feeling a little embarrassed.

"Yes, you are," Bonnie insisted. "Teach us that dance where you wriggle your shoulders. And the one where you step back and fling your arms up like this." Bonnie flicked up her hands, and knocked a lamp off the table.

"This could be dangerous," said Shane. "I'm in."

Lucy put the CD player on. It had marks all over it, and it couldn't go very loud, but with everyone singing along it sounded OK.

Lucy decided Tom was a pretty good dancer for a boy. She showed him the

moves, and he copied them. He even had a little of his own style. He kept on flipping his hair back as he danced. It really matched the song.

It was much harder teaching Shane and Bonnie the moves. When Lucy told them to take three steps to the right, they went to the left. When she asked them to shake their shoulders and snap their fingers, they couldn't seem to do both at the same time.

Lucy secretly decided to give Shane and Bonnie the easy parts, but they didn't seem to notice.

They liked the part where they leaped out from behind the curtains, tapping their feet. The only problem was that they kept leaping out too quickly, and landing in the wrong spot!

After they bumped into Lucy and Tom

for the tenth time, Lucy put two pieces of paper on the carpet to show them where they should end up. On the eleventh try, it actually worked.

It was fantastic having four people to direct. Now that Frankie had decided she was too grown up to join in, Lucy usually just looked in the mirror while she practiced her dances at home.

After about an hour of practicing, the show was ready.

Ross and Helen came in to watch the performance. It went really well—except

for the part where Bonnie and Shane knocked their heads together really hard.

As they took their bows, Ross and Helen clapped wildly.

"That was terrific, you guys," Ross said. "Maybe we should get rid of the television at home, too. It makes you all so much more creative!"

Shane's eyes nearly popped out of their sockets.

"No way!" he said.

He looked so panicked at the idea of not having a TV that everyone laughed out loud.

Soon, Lucy and Bonnie were all tucked in bed.

It had been a great day, and Lucy thought about writing in her new diary.

Should I write in my diary?

But she couldn't find the energy to get it out of her bag. In her head, she said good night to her mom and dad, and then to Frankie. She did miss them a little, but she didn't feel sad.

Bonnie's voice drifted up from the bottom bunk.

"Hey, what about Mia? Don't you think she's weird? I think Karen's nice, though. I can't wait until tomorrow. We are going to . . ."

Soon, Bonnie's voice was just a part of Lucy's dream.

CHAPTER FIVE

"Can we trade wetsuits?" Lucy asked when they got to the beach the next morning.

"Why?" Bonnie asked.

"Well, I just thought that maybe your wetsuit would fit me better," Lucy answered.

In her dream, she had been riding the waves like a pro surfer. And in her dream, she was *definitely* wearing Bonnie's wetsuit with the green swirls.

"Sure," Bonnie said, peeling off the wetsuit and throwing it to Lucy. "But they are exactly the same size."

Luke walked over to the girls just as they were zipping up their wetsuits.

"Hey, grommets. How's it hanging?" asked Luke.

"Good," Bonnie and Lucy replied, giggling. Luke really talked like a surfer.

Lucy was so excited. She felt like she was about to shock Luke and the others in class. They would not believe how much better she was surfing in the green swirly wetsuit.

It would be just like in her dream.

The group ran out into the ocean.

Lucy lay flat on her tummy on the board, and steered it through the swell. She was ready to try out what Luke had taught them.

Lucy tried to jump from her belly to her knees. On the first try, she managed to get one knee on the board. But the other knee slipped off, and the rest of Lucy followed.

She tried again. This time, she counted. One, two, three, *up*.

Both knees were on the board, but only for a second. Lucy lost her balance, and fell into the water with a big splash.

She wasn't going to give up, though. On the third try, both of Lucy's knees landed on the board, and they stayed there! Lucy was kneeling! She was really doing it.

She felt the board move under her, gliding through the water.

This feels fantastic!

It was fantastic.

"Bonnie, look at me!" she called. Lucy turned her head to look for Bonnie. She was probably under the water somewhere. Finally, Lucy hopped off the board. She was breathing heavily.

"Well done, grommet," said Luke. "And look at your friend out there. She's a natural."

Lucy put her hand up to shield her eyes from the sun. She looked out, far into the water.

First, she noticed that Karen was out where the waves broke. As she watched, Karen actually *stood* on her board. Lucy clapped. Karen was amazing.

She wanted Bonnie to see what was happening. She glanced around the shore-line, searching for Bonnie. She started to get worried when she couldn't see her anywhere. She was just about to tell Luke, when she looked out at the water again.

Bonnie was *standing* on her board,

riding a big wave! She twisted and turned through the surf. For a moment, she disappeared inside the tunnel of the wave. Then she came out the other end, looking wobbly but still standing! It was incredible.

Luke put his fingers in his mouth and whistled loudly.

"Nice surfing," he called out. "Gee, that Bonnie has talent," he said to Lucy. "Isn't she great?"

"Totally great," Lucy agreed.

Just then, Lucy realized that Mia had come up beside her. It seemed kind of spooky to Lucy, the way Mia did that. It would be OK if she talked, but she hardly ever said a word.

At the end of the lesson, the four girls sat on the beach in front of Luke. He had a piece of paper in his hand.

"You guys did really well today," he said. "A couple of you even did well enough to go up to the next level."

Lucy held her breath. She *was* doing better with her kneeling. Maybe, just maybe . . .

"Bonnie and Karen, you will be moving up into Aaron's group," said Luke.

Bonnie and Karen squealed, and gave each other a high five.

"Mia and Lucy, you guys are stuck with

me for another lesson," he said. He ruffled Lucy's hair, and gave her a friendly wink.

Luke was a really great teacher.

So why did Lucy feel so miserable?

I will never be as good as Bonnie!

CHAPTER SIX

That afternoon, Lucy lay her towel down on the sand next to Helen's beach chair. Ross's feet stuck out of the end of their sun tent. Lucy could tell where Tom got his snoring from.

"Wanna play soccer?" Bonnie called, squeezing her wet hair onto Lucy's hot, dry back.

"No," said Lucy, getting out her book.

"I'm just going to read for a while."

Lucy tried to get into her book. It was an exciting part, but she couldn't concentrate. She read the same page three times before she gave up and lay her head down on the towel.

"Are you OK, sweetie?" Helen asked. "Would you like some juice?"

"No, thanks, I'm fine," Lucy replied, trying to sound happy.

But she didn't *feel* fine. It was hard to explain exactly what she felt. She was sad, for sure, about Bonnie going up a level in surfing class. It meant that they wouldn't be together. The whole idea of this vacation was that they would learn to surf together!

And now Lucy was going to be stuck with Mia in beginners.

It wasn't fair.

I know I should feel happy for Bonnie.

She couldn't help it if she wasn't as good as Bonnie. She felt like she was being punished, having to stay down while Bonnie went up to a higher level.

"Sweetheart, if you want to talk about anything with me, you can," Helen said kindly.

"Thanks," Lucy said quickly, "but everything's fine."

She didn't want to talk about her feelings with Bonnie's mom. It was all too confusing. She would probably end up saying the wrong thing, and Helen would make a big deal out of it. Or she would worry that Bonnie was being mean to her.

"You know," said Lucy, getting up off

her towel, "I might play soccer with the others after all."

She raced off to join the others.

"You're in luck," Bonnie said, as Lucy joined them. "We've finished the soccer game. Now we're playing hide and seek. You can go anywhere between the beach shack and the trampolines. I'm it."

Bonnie put her hands over her eyes and started counting. The boys scattered. Lucy ran up a sand dune and squatted inside a bush. It was a good hiding place. She was out of the hot sun and she could see between the leaves.

She sat there and waited. It seemed like ages before Bonnie walked in her direction.

She had already found Shane, and he was helping her find the others. Lucy tried to stay perfectly still. Then she heard Shane's voice.

"What's wrong with Lucy today?" he asked Bonnie.

"Nothing's wrong. What do you mean?" Bonnie asked.

"Well, she's really quiet."

"I guess she's a *little* bit quiet today."

"Maybe she's angry about something?"

"What would she be angry about?" Bonnie asked, looking under a picnic table to see if anyone was hiding there.

"I don't know, maybe she's jealous that you moved up a level in surfing."

Lucy held her breath.

"Lucy isn't like that," Bonnie said angrily. "She wouldn't be *jealous* I'm moving up a level. She'd be *happy* for me."

Their voices were getting softer. They had walked right by Lucy's hiding spot.

Lucy finally let out a sigh.

Maybe she *was* jealous?

She felt terrible. How could she be jealous of her best friend? She just would not let herself feel that way. She would *make* herself feel happy for Bonnie, even if she did have to stay in the beginners' class with Mia.

Suddenly, Lucy felt homesick.

It was strange. She had always thought

that if she got homesick it would be at nighttime, when she was tucked into someone else's bed, with somebody else's family down the hallway. She had *never* imagined that she would feel homesick in the middle of the day. Or while she was hiding inside a bush!

She wished she could see Frankie, or her mom. At least then she could talk honestly about her feelings.

She thought about what Frankie had said about writing in a diary. Lucy would write about this bad feeling so it would escape out of her head and onto the pages of the diary. Then everything would go back to normal.

CHAPTER
SEVEN

When they got back from the beach, Lucy sneaked into the bedroom. She took out the diary and its tiny key from her backpack. Then she climbed up to the top bunk and pulled the blanket over her, like a tent. She had to leave a hole for air, and for light.

At first, it was hard to put her feelings into words. But she really wanted to get this bad feeling out of her. She was

worried it was making her mean on the inside. Soon, Lucy was writing away.

It did make her feel better!

Lucy was so busy writing that she didn't hear Bonnie walk into the bedroom.

"What are you doing, Lou?" Bonnie asked. "Is that a game? I'll come in with you, and we can pretend we're camping."

Lucy looked through the hole in the blanket.

"I'm just resting," she said. Bonnie climbed up the ladder to the top bunk and pulled back the blanket.

"What's that book then?" she asked.

Lucy shut the diary quickly, and locked it.

"It's nothing. It's just my diary," she replied.

"Can I see?" Bonnie asked.

Lucy shook her head. There was *no way* she wanted Bonnie to read what she had written.

"It's actually private," Lucy explained.

"I won't tell anyone," Bonnie said. "Anyway, we're best friends. We shouldn't have secrets from each other."

Lucy tucked the diary under her pillow. She kept the key in her hand.

"It's not about secrets," Lucy said. "I just wrote a little about what happened to me on this vacation."

"Then you must have written about

things that have happened to me as well, because we're on this vacation together," Bonnie pleaded. "Please? Please with sugar on top? Let me read it."

"Don't worry about my diary," she said. "It's only boring stuff." She slid down the ladder onto the floor. "Why don't we play hide and seek outside?"

"Come on, Lou. Now I'm going to wonder about—" Bonnie stopped as Helen called out.

"Hey, you girls. Come downstairs. I want to talk to you about something."

Thank goodness for Bonnie's mom, thought Lucy, as they turned to go downstairs. Lucy felt like she'd been saved.

"We'd better go," she said. "It sounds important."

Bonnie gave her a funny look as she walked out the door.

Lucy ran back to her backpack and dropped the key in the front pocket.

She didn't notice that Bonnie had also turned back, and was peeking at Lucy's hiding place for the key.

CHAPTER EIGHT

"Let's have a big barbeque tomorrow night," said Helen, when they got downstairs. "You can invite the girls from your surfing class. The twins are going to ask a couple of kids as well."

Bonnie seemed to have forgotten about the diary. She looked really happy.

"Wicked," she said. "Let's put on a *gigantic* concert. Lucy can teach everyone the moves. I hope Karen can come."

Lucy felt that bad feeling drift through her mind. She imagined Bonnie and Karen dancing and having fun together, while she was stuck sitting in the corner with Mia.

"What about that girl in your level, Lucy?" Helen asked. It felt like she was reading Lucy's mind.

"Oh, we don't have to ask Mia," Lucy said.

"Well, I don't think you should leave her out. You might hurt her feelings," said Helen. Lucy nodded.

"OK, that would be nice," she said. She didn't want Helen to think she was the kind of girl who liked to hurt people's

feelings. Anyway, she would just make sure she was included with Bonnie and Karen, so it didn't really matter. And she was determined to improve at surfing lessons tomorrow. Maybe she would get to move up a level, too.

Everything would work out.

The next morning, Lucy watched as Karen and Bonnie walked along the beach with their new teacher. They had their heads together, and she heard a tinkle of laughter drift back towards her.

"Hi," she said to Mia, as they both walked

towards Luke.

"Hello, Lucy," Mia mumbled, looking down at her feet.

As they walked into the water, Lucy tried to concentrate. She lay down on her board and paddled. The waves were bigger today, and it was harder to get over them. But she was going to do it. She felt Mia follow at her heels.

"Hey, Lucy, don't forget to smile," Luke said.

Lucy didn't feel like smiling. She shot him a fake grin. Luke grinned back at her, but his smile was for real. Lucy felt her face relax, and soon she was giving him a real smile.

"Phew, that's better!" he said. "Now, up on your knees, girls."

Lucy took a deep breath. She jumped off her feet and landed on her knees the first time!

She felt the movement of the ocean under her. She rose slowly, from her knees to her feet. She was surfing!

It felt amazing. Lucy looked around. Mia was in front of her, clapping.

The next thing she knew, she was underneath a swirl of water. She felt the pull of the leash around her ankle. She tried to twist her way up to the top of the water.

Her board was above her, coming towards her head. Lucy covered her face, and got ready for the bump.

But it didn't come.

Instead, Mia grabbed the board and

held it away from her. Lucy rose to the surface safely.

"Hey, thanks for that, Mia," she said, gasping for breath.

Mia grinned. Lucy noticed that her whole face changed with that grin. She looked like a different person.

"That's OK," Mia said. "You were awesome, Lucy!"

Lucy giggled. "It *was* awesome!" she said. "You have to try it."

Soon, Lucy and Mia were riding the waves together. Mia was trying really hard. At the end of each ride, they talked with Luke about how to make the next one better. It was a lot of fun.

The lesson went so quickly that Lucy couldn't believe it when their time was up.

Afterwards, they waited on the beach for Bonnie and Karen.

"Mia, we are having a barbeque tonight," Lucy said. "It would be great if you could come."

CHAPTER NINE

They were having hamburgers and hot dogs for the barbeque. Ross put on a funny apron with "World's Best Chef" written on the front.

Lucy and Bonnie helped Helen make red Jell-O for dessert.

Then they went into the playroom to decide on what music they would use for their concert.

"Karen really likes Jesse Black," Bonnie said. "Let's make up a dance to one of his songs."

"He's not that great to dance to," Lucy replied. "I think we should choose someone else."

"What about Kayla Storm?" Bonnie asked. "I think Karen likes Kayla as well."

Lucy sighed. She couldn't really say that Kayla wasn't good to dance to. But somehow, that's what she wanted to say.

"I don't think Mia likes Kayla," she said.

It was weird. She didn't know why she said that—Lucy had no idea what kind of music Mia liked.

Bonnie looked puzzled.

I don't know
why I said that.

"How would you know what Mia likes?" she said. "She hardly talks!"

"She *does* talk," Lucy replied. "She's just shy at first. She's actually really nice."

Bonnie shrugged. "OK, then. Let's just choose something *we* like," she said.

"Good idea," said Lucy.

The CD player in the car was much more powerful than the one in the playroom, so Bonnie and Lucy decided to use that instead. The back door of the car was open, and music pumped through the air.

The front yard looked amazing. Shane and Tom had strung lights in the trees. As it got dark, the lights started to glow.

Karen and Mia arrived at the same time. It was strange seeing them out of their wetsuits.

Lucy thought Mia looked beautiful. She had her hair up in a high ponytail, and she had a little bit of glitter on her eyelids. She ran straight up to Lucy.

"This looks awesome," Mia said, grinning.

The twins' friends arrived just as Helen started serving the hot dogs and

hamburgers. It was delicious, but the red Jell-O for dessert was even yummier.

After dinner, the kids all went outside.

"Are we going to put on one of your dumb concerts?" Tom asked.

Bonnie nudged him. "If they're so dumb, you don't have to join in," she said.

Tom shrugged. "I think I *have* to," he said. "You girls would be lost without me. The concert would be too boring."

He did a little twist and shimmy to prove his point. Bonnie, Shane, and Lucy jumped on him and started tickling him.

"Say 'Lucy is the best dancer, and her concerts are fantastic'," Bonnie insisted, as the others held Tom down.

Everyone was laughing so hard that they almost missed what Tom said.

"OK!" Tom panted, still trying to get the others off him. "Lucy is the best dancer."

It was so much fun tickling Tom that Lucy didn't notice everyone else had stopped.

"Hey, Lou, you can stop now," Bonnie teased.

Lucy felt a bit embarrassed.

"OK, let's dance!" she said.

There were a lot of people to teach, but that only made it more fun. It was like having her own dance class. She showed them all the moves, and they copied in their own way.

Finally, the concert was ready. Ross and Helen and a few of their friends came outside to watch.

Let's dance!

Dancing in the moonlight was beautiful. Lucy felt the warm air whoosh over her as she moved. She felt the music flow through her, and all the moves seemed to happen without even trying.

She could tell that Tom felt the music,

too. Even though he was using most of the moves Lucy had taught him, there was something extra in the way he danced.

Mia was pretty good, too, but everyone else looked a little bit like robots compared to Tom. Lucy actually found herself copying some of *his* moves.

Lucy felt proud as she watched her friends doing the dance she had made up. But it wasn't because it looked good. Bonnie really was a terrible dancer, but in some ways she was having the most fun because she didn't care how she looked.

Lucy's face ached from all the smiling. She wished the night would last forever, but it seemed like the shortest night in history.

By the time the concert was over, it was really late. Everybody had to go home.

Bonnie must have been exhausted, because she was really quick to go to bed. Lucy chatted with Tom for a while before she went to bed.

She was still smiling as she brushed her teeth. As she walked into the bedroom, she was thinking of all the things she wanted to say to Bonnie about their fantastic evening.

But Bonnie wasn't in her bed.

Lucy looked around the room. It took her a minute to realize that Bonnie was up in her bunk, with the blanket pulled over her like a tent.

Lucy held her breath. Something was wrong—she could feel it in her bones.

Lucy climbed up the ladder to the top bunk and looked under the blanket. Bonnie's angry eyes looked back at her. Then Lucy noticed what she was doing.

Bonnie was reading her diary!

CHAPTER TEN

Lucy crawled inside the blanket tent with Bonnie.

"Are you OK?" she asked, feeling bad.

Bonnie shook her head. "No. But at least I know what you are *really* thinking now. No wonder you wanted your diary to be a secret."

Lucy bit her lip.

This was going to be hard.

"I'm sorry, Bonnie," she blurted out. "I know I had some bad feelings about you moving up a level in surfing class. I was all mixed up. I *am* proud of you. You are incredible. You're always like that. You just try something, and all of a sudden, you're great at it. I guess I was a little jealous."

Bonnie threw back the blanket.

"Well, *you're* good at some things that I'm hopeless at," she said. "What about dancing? I've still got a bruise on my head from when I banged into Shane!"

Lucy didn't say anything for a moment. She just thought about what Bonnie had said. It was true!

"You're right, Bonnie," she said. "It wasn't

I should never have felt jealous of my best friend.

fair of me to get jealous. But it wasn't only about the surfing. It was also that you and Karen were getting along so well, and I felt kind of left out. I wanted us to be doing everything together on this vacation."

The anger in Bonnie's eyes melted.

"Lou, you are my best friend," she said. "Nothing would change that."

Lucy felt a tear slide down her cheek. Bonnie grabbed hold of her hand.

"You are so silly," she said gently.

"I *am* silly," Lucy agreed.

"Promise you'll tell me how you feel from now on, instead of just writing about it in your diary?" Bonnie asked.

Lucy hugged her friend.

"I promise," she said.

CHAPTER ELEVEN

The vacation was almost over. Only one more night, and then Lucy would be back home with her family.

She felt a little sad—she was getting used to being part of the Preston family. She could tell that Bonnie felt a little sad, too. Even Shane and Tom were quiet. Nobody wanted to put on a concert. Nobody wanted to play hide and seek or soccer.

They sat on the front porch. They could see a beam of light coming from the lighthouse and travelling far out to sea.

"It's great that you moved up a level in surfing today," Bonnie said.

Both Lucy and Mia had finally left Luke's class, and gone into Aaron's class.

Lucy gave Bonnie a friendly shove. "Yeah, except that you and Karen moved up another level, too," she laughed. "I don't think I'll ever get to be in the same class as you."

"Next year you will," Bonnie replied.

"Can I come again next year?" Lucy asked, brightening.

"Yes, doofus! Of course you can."

"Then I don't care whether I'm in the same group as you or not. We can all hang out together after classes anyway."

"Hang on a minute," said Shane. "Next year it should be me or Tom who gets to bring a friend. Isn't that right, Tom?"

Tom was sitting next to Lucy.

"Nah, I'm happy for Lou to come again," he said quietly, looking right at Lucy.

Lucy felt her heart beating. It was so loud she wondered if the others could hear it. Luckily, no one seemed to notice.

"Dinner, surfer kids!" Helen called out.

Shane and Bonnie charged inside. They were *always* hungry.

Lucy and Tom followed a minute later, to see Ross putting on his silly apron again.

"Voilà," he said, with his best French accent. "For you hungry beasts, I present my famous chicken cutlets, roast potatoes, and broccoli."

"Dad, Lucy *hates* broccoli," Bonnie

said. "It makes her want to spew. She doesn't have to eat it, does she?"

Lucy smiled at her friend. She was so glad things were back to normal.

Ross shook his head. "Lucy, you don't have to eat your broccoli. Although I do think you should try just a *little* bit."

Lucy found herself doing something she thought she would never do. She put a piece of potato and chicken on her fork. Then she squished a little bit of broccoli into it. She put the food into her mouth and chewed.

"Lucy!" Bonnie exclaimed. "What are you doing?"

"I'm having a little taste," Lucy said.

"What do you think?" Bonnie asked, as Lucy swallowed the mouthful.

"Actually, it's not too bad," she said, smiling.

Dear Diary,

Nothing much has changed at home.

It's funny, because it seemed like a long time to be away, and I feel different. I even have a real-life secret! I'm going to write about it, but I'm also going to hide the key to this diary somewhere VERY safe. Because this is PRIVATE.

Last night, when Bonnie and Shane went inside for dinner, Tom reminded me about the first day of the vacation, when I got seaweed *around my neck in the water. That day, he told me I looked like a sea monster. Then he got really quiet and whispered that I actually looked like a mermaid.*

I wonder what that means?

I can't wait to tell Bonnie.

Anyway, I found a picture in a magazine of the wetsuit I want, and I've already started saving for it. It has little pink stripes down the sleeves. It's even nicer than Bonnie's green swirly wetsuit. And I really think it might make me surf even better next year!

THE END

Sophie makes a new friend when she is moved to the other class at school. But Sophie's best friend doesn't get along with the new girl in Sophie's life. With school camp coming up, will Sophie be forced to choose between her new bestie and her old bestie?

Keep reading for an excerpt!

CHAPTER ✲ ONE

"OK, everyone," called Mr. Perelli above the noise. "Ten more problems to do in the last ten minutes!"

Sophie groaned.

This was the longest math lesson *ever*. Usually Sophie liked math, but today she couldn't concentrate.

"I wish the bell would ring," she whispered to her friend Alice.

"Me, too!" replied Alice. "I've got to finish packing for tomorrow."

Sophie felt a shiver of excitement. Tomorrow they were going to school camp. They were staying near a lake and would be going canoeing. Best of all, they were camping overnight!

"I wish it was just our class going," said Marie, who sat nearby. "Mrs. Tran's class

I can't wait to go camping!

is really stuck up. They're going to hate camping!"

"They'll probably freak out if they get a tiny bit of mud on them!" said Alice, laughing.

Sophie didn't know what to say. The thing is, she used to be in Mrs. Tran's class. She started school with those kids and she got to know them all really well. Her best friend Megan is in Mrs. Tran's class.

Sophie and Megan had always thought they would go right through school together. But two months ago the teachers decided to move some kids from each class. Sophie didn't know if she was excited or scared when Mrs. Tran told her she was one of them. Probably a little of both. Everyone in Mrs. Tran's class said that Mr. Perelli's class was rough and mean.

"The boys catch bugs," Megan said, wrinkling her nose. "Then they eat them."

"The girls hang from the monkey bars even when they're wearing dresses," said Katie. "They don't care if their undies are showing."

"And Mr. Perelli yells *all* the time," added Claire.

Chloe's nervous about going back to school. To make matters worse, this new math is so, so, so difficult. Is everyone else really smarter than Chloe?

Keep reading for an excerpt!

CHAPTER
ONE

I stood on stage, under the spotlight. Even though the rest of the concert hall was in darkness, I knew that it was full of people, watching me. But I wasn't nervous at all. I'd practiced this dance routine hundreds of times. I knew I wouldn't make a mistake.

The music started and I began dancing. My costume trailed behind me like mist as I moved. I had to be careful that I didn't step on it. It would be terrible to fall over in front of all these people. But I didn't fall, even when the music got really fast.

The hardest part was toward the end when I had to spin five times in a row, then jump into the air. I started spinning and the spotlight followed me across the stage. By the third twirl I knew everything was going to be OK.

I finished with the splits and the crowd went wild. They rose to their feet and cheered. My best friend, Dani, ran on to the stage and gave me a big hug.

"That was really cool, Chloe," she said.

As she spoke, the concert hall and all the people disappeared.

We were in Dani's living room.

"I think our dance routine is looking great," Dani added.

"Me, too," I said.

Dani and I had been working on this routine all summer. Dani took dance lessons, so she worked out most of it. But I had made up a few steps, too, which Dani said were really good.

After our practice, we were both pooped. We flopped down on the floor, still in our costumes. Dani's mom had given us a bag of old stuff to use. I was wearing a soft silky dress covered in tiny gold beads. It was excellent to dance in because it swirled out around me when

I spun. Dani's outfit was a satin skirt with a zebra pattern. It was too big so to keep it up she had on a wide stretchy belt.

"Can you believe it's the last day of summer vacation?" said Dani.

I shook my head. "This summer has gone so fast," I said.

"I'm actually looking forward to going back," Dani admitted. "Is that weird?"

I knew what she meant. It had been a great vacation, but I was also excited about going back to school.

Everything was going to change this year. We were moving to a whole new area, where the older kids go. There would be different classrooms and different

I'm actually looking forward to going back to school!

bathrooms. There would even be a different playground. It was almost like starting at a new school.

"But I'm a little nervous, too," Dani said. "Everyone says the work will be much harder now. Especially math."

I got butterflies in my stomach when she said that. Math wasn't exactly my best subject. I had done OK in Mrs. Khan's class last year, but the work was pretty easy.

"I think it depends on which teacher you get," I said. "Mr. Stavros is nice, but Mrs. Clarke is really strict."

My big sister, Ashley, used to go to the same school as me. She'd told me all about the teachers.

"Mr. Stavros gives out stickers if you do good work," she said. "But Mrs. Clarke only ever gives check marks. And no one ever gets more than one check."

I wanted to be in Mr. Stavros's class. He played guitar and gave his kids silly nicknames. There was a boy in his class last year called Alec Jamieson but Mr. Stavros called him "I-lick-jam-and-scones." It was kind of dumb, but it was funny, too.

Mrs. Clarke always called kids by their proper names. She didn't even shorten them. If your name was Samantha, that's what she'd call you, even if everyone else called you Ant.

But there was another reason I didn't

want Mrs. Clarke to be my teacher. It was because of something bad that happened last year.

I was playing four square and I ran backward to hit the ball. I didn't notice Mrs. Clarke standing right behind me, and I knocked her over.

I mean, *completely* over.

I turned around and there she was, flat on her back, looking really surprised. I was worried she was hurt but she got up and brushed herself off.

"I'm sorry, Mrs. Clarke," I said nervously.

I thought she'd say something like, *That's OK, I know you didn't mean it*. That's what Mrs. Khan would've said. But she didn't.

Go Girl!

If you loved this story, don't miss the rest of the series!